Molly and the Friendly Seagulls

Written and illustrated by

STEPHEN DUNNE

ISBN: 9798849861746

DEDICATED

To Sole and Lily

ACKNOWLEDGMENTS

Thank you, Martin, for helping me to put this book together.

One hot day during the summer holidays, Molly and her Nan decided to take a day trip to the seaside.

Nan made up a picnic basket full of Molly's favorite treats before they set off on a minibus for the hour-long journey. Molly was very excited, as it had been a long time since she had been to the seaside.

Of course, Nan had to bring her scooter, so it was a special minibus that arrived to take them to the seaside. Molly made sure that she also took a bucket and spade to build castles on the sand.

Once Molly and Nan were seated on the minibus, the driver asked: *"Are you both ready to set off on your adventure?"*

"YES PLEASE!" they both shouted.

They sang songs and chatted as they were driven through the countryside. Before long, the minibus stopped by the beach huts. They had arrived!

The driver unloaded Nan's scooter and said: ***"Have a good time at the beach!"***

He explained that he would return later to collect them both and take them home. He waved goodbye.

Nan found it difficult to bring the scooter onto the sand as the wheels kept getting stuck. She decided to stay by a bench on the boardwalk where she could look out at the sea.

Nan told Molly to put the picnic blanket on the sand just in front of the bench.

Molly played and built sandcastles while Nan read a book under her big sun hat.

A little while later, Nan asked Molly to unpack the picnic basket because they were both getting hungry. Molly sat next to Nan on the bench, where they both began to enjoy the picnic.

Suddenly, a seagull swooped down from the roof of a nearby beach hut and landed a few feet from where they were sitting. At first, Molly was annoyed. She tried to shoo the seagull away.

"Don't worry, these seagulls are friendly!" said Nan.

So, Molly relaxed and carried on munching her crisps.

The seagull walked towards Molly.

"Hello! My name is Sid."

Molly looked at him in surprise. She had never heard a seagull talk before.

"Do you have any food you could share with me?"

Before Molly could say anything, another seagull swooped down and landed next to Sid.

"Hi - I'm Sherry!" said the new seagull.

"Hello!" replied Molly in amazement.

Molly turned and looked at Nan, who gave Molly a big smile.

Nan said: *"Don't worry, Molly. I know Sid and Sherry very well.*

That's why they landed near us. Would you like to give them some of our food?"

Molly fed both seagulls. They gobbled it up quickly.

Molly giggled and Nan laughed as both birds squabbled over the food.

Molly chatted for some time with Sid and Sherry. She told them about her two friends Nelly and Ben, the donkeys at the animal sanctuary.

She wondered if they would both like to visit the sanctuary.

"You should stay for a night or two to see what life is like at the sanctuary!" said Molly.

Sid and Sherry thought this was a great idea. They asked if there was plenty of food at the sanctuary because they would be very hungry after taking the long flight to get there.

Molly assured them that there was plenty of food for any visitor to the sanctuary.

Nan told Molly that it was time to pack up the picnic basket as the minibus driver would soon return to take them home.

Molly packed up the picnic basket and gave Sid and Sherry the food that had not yet been eaten.

They were delighted.

The minibus soon arrived. It was empty, so Molly could sit wherever she wanted. The driver put Nan's scooter, the empty picnic basket and Molly's bucket and spade onto the minibus and they were off!

Molly soon noticed that Sid was flying close to the window. She told Sid to be careful as he might get hurt flying so close to the minibus.

Sid shouted through the window: *"I don't know how to get to the animal sanctuary!*

Please can you give me the directions?

"Yes - of course!" said Molly.

Sid thanked Molly and flew back to Sherry.

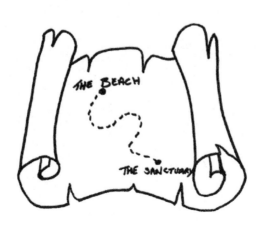

On their way home, Molly wondered if it really was such a good idea for Sid and Sherry to visit. After all, they were quite greedy seagulls. They seemed to be hungry all the time and gobbled up their food really quickly.

Nan explained to Molly that all animals were different and that this was just Sid and Sherry's nature. The other animals in the sanctuary would know how to deal with them if they became too greedy.

This put Molly's mind to rest, and she soon fell asleep beside Nan.

Molly had enjoyed a lovely day playing in the sand, eating the picnic treats and getting to know Sid and Sherry.

Nan didn't wake Molly up until they had arrived back home.

OTHER BOOKS IN THIS SERIES

Book 1: Molly and the Lonely Donkey

Book 2: Molly and the Friendly Seagulls

Book 3: Molly and the Pretty Pony

Book 4: Molly's Gold Star

Book 5: Molly's Bright Idea

MOLLY AND THE FRIENDLY SEAGULLS

ABOUT THE AUTHOR

Stephen Dunne is an accomplished artist. Born and raised in rural Ireland and now living on the Kent coast in England, he is very influenced by nature and wildlife. This is the second adventure with Molly and her friends.

Printed in Great Britain
by Amazon

46166520R00020